This Walker book belongs to:

_____

_____

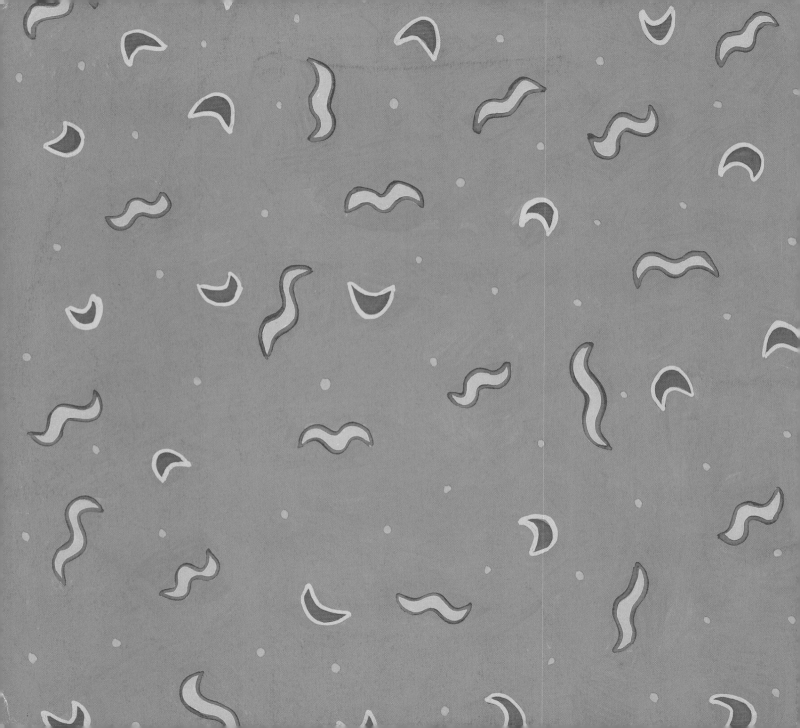

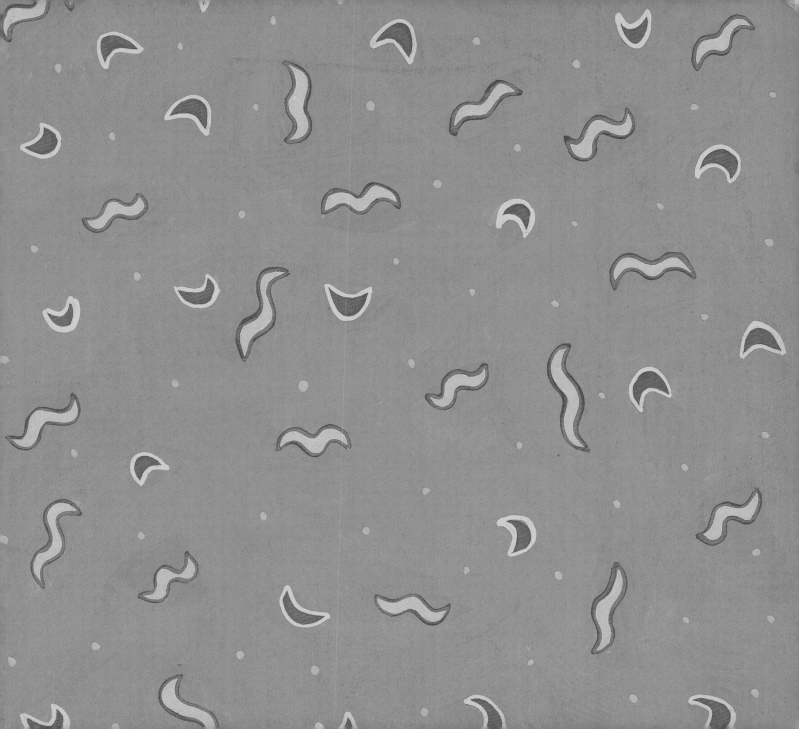

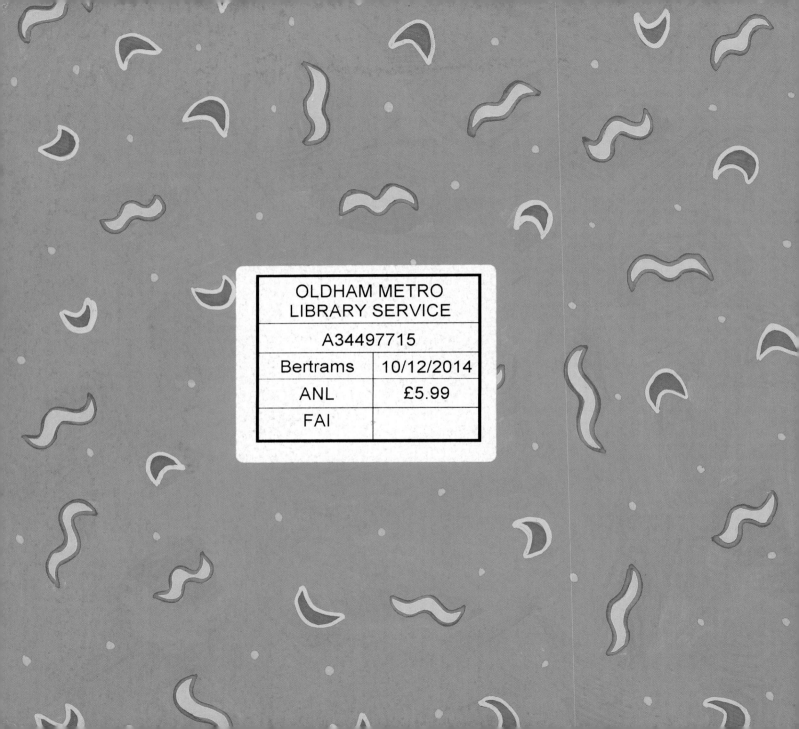

HELPING LITTLE STAR

Sally Morgan and Blaze Kwaymullina

ILLUSTRATIONS BY SALLY MORGAN

WALKER BOOKS
AND SUBSIDIARIES

LONDON • BOSTON • SYDNEY • AUCKLAND

"Do not go near the edge of Night Sky,"
warned Moon, "or you will fall off."

But Little Star didn't listen.

Down, down, down he fell.
SPLASH!

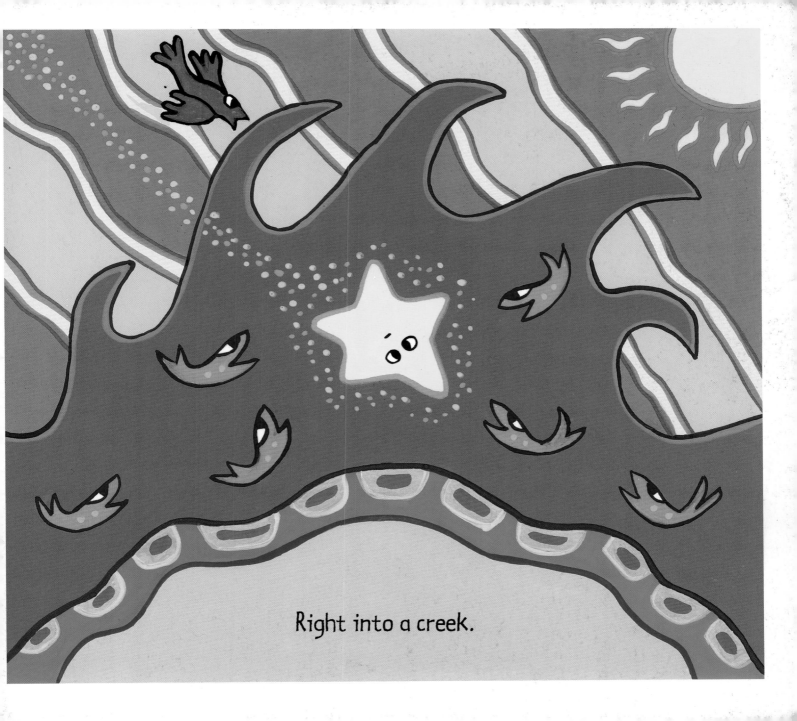

Right into a creek.

"What are you doing in my
swimming hole?" asked Python.
"I fell off Night Sky," cried Little Star.
"Can you help me get home?"

Coiling his tail, Python flicked
Little Star out of the water.

THUD!
Right into a cave.

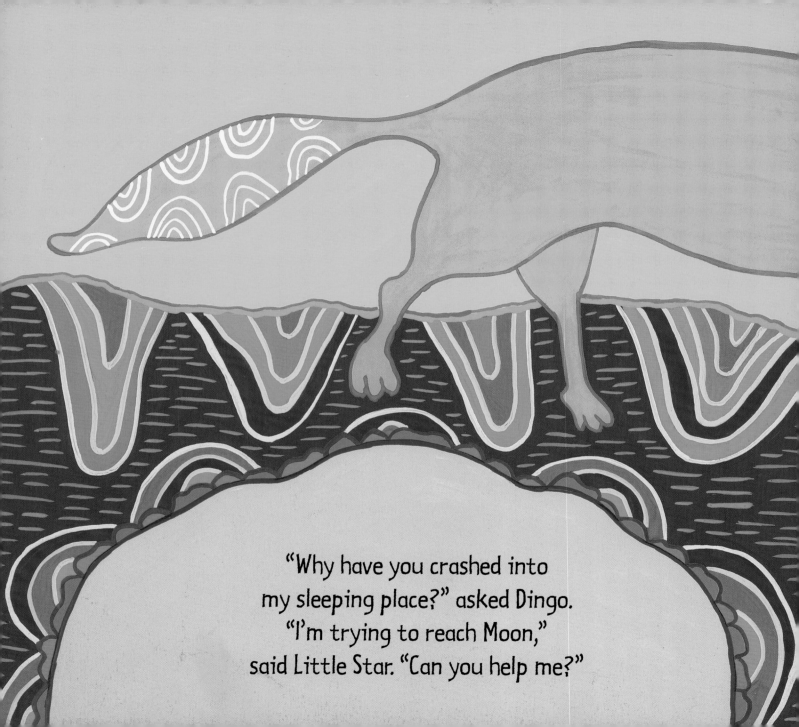

"Why have you crashed into
my sleeping place?" asked Dingo.
"I'm trying to reach Moon,"
said Little Star. "Can you help me?"

Scrambling outside, Dingo tossed
Little Star into the air.

OOMPH!
Right into a soft furry pouch.

"I only have one joey,"
said Mother Kangaroo. "Who are you?"
"I'm Little Star," he said.
"And I'm lost!"

Mother Kangaroo called Dingo and
Python to come and help.
"If we climb Big Hill," she said,
"we can help Little Star get home."

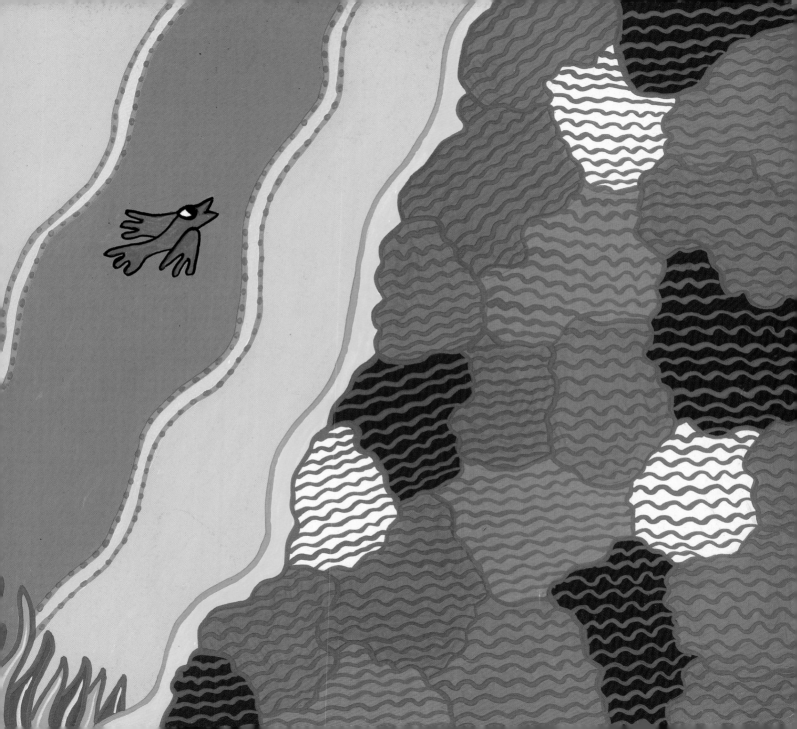

So the animals climbed Big Hill and
they stretched and stretched and stretched ...

Until ... PLOP!
Little Star fell back into Night Sky.

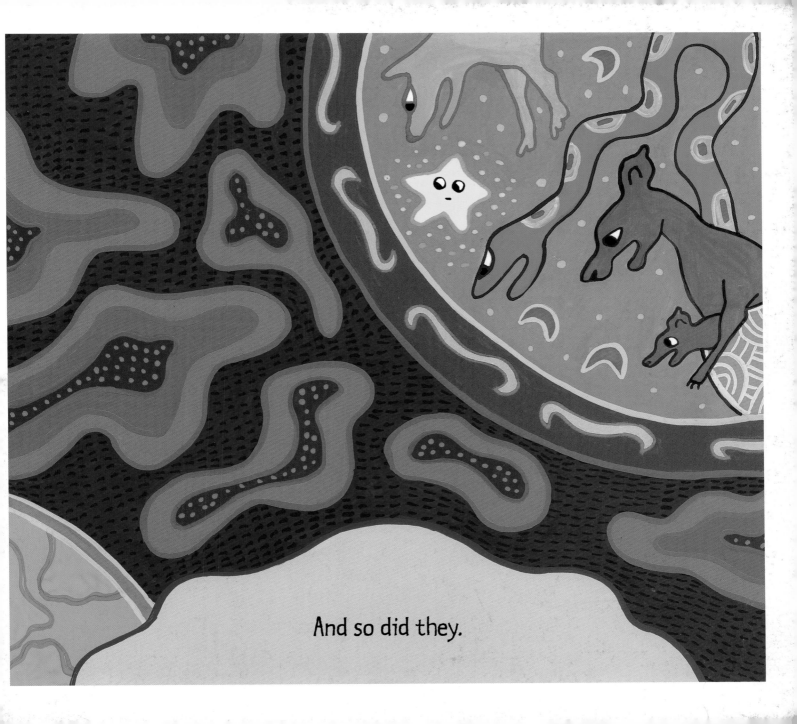

And so did they.

Moon laughed. "Thank you for
bringing my Little Star home," she said.
"Now it's my turn to help you."

Then SWOOSH.
Moon sent them tumbling
back to Earth in a river of moonlight.
"Oh, Moon," said Little Star.
"I'm so glad to be home!"

First published 2013 by Walker Books Ltd
87 Vauxhall Walk, London SE11 5HJ

This edition published 2014

2 4 6 8 10 9 7 5 3 1

Text © 2013 Sally Morgan and Blaze Kwaymullina
Illustrations © 2013 Sally Morgan

This book has been typeset in Kosmik

Printed in China

British Library Cataloguing in Publication Data:
a catalogue record for this book is available from the British Library

ISBN 978-1-4063-5530-7

www.walker.co.uk

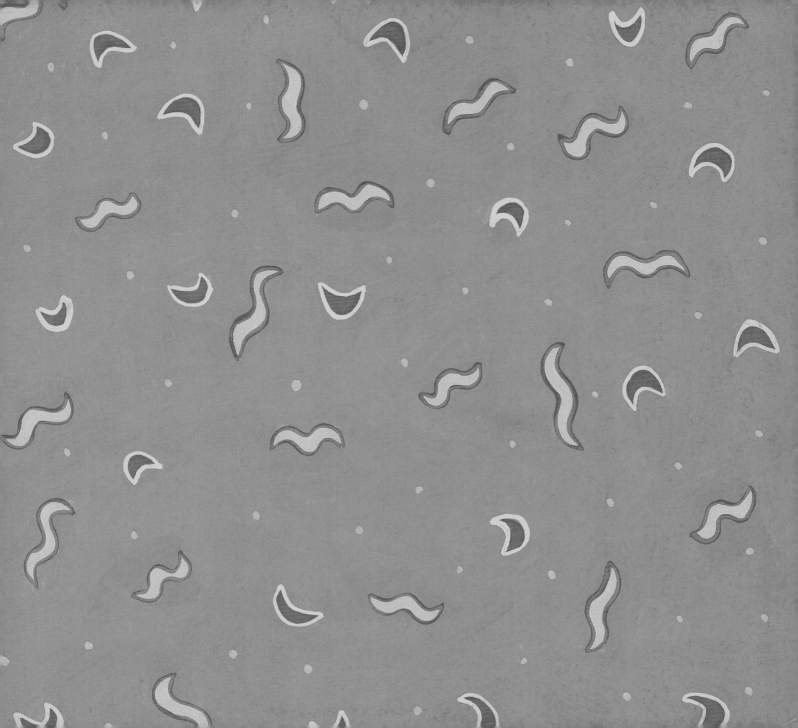

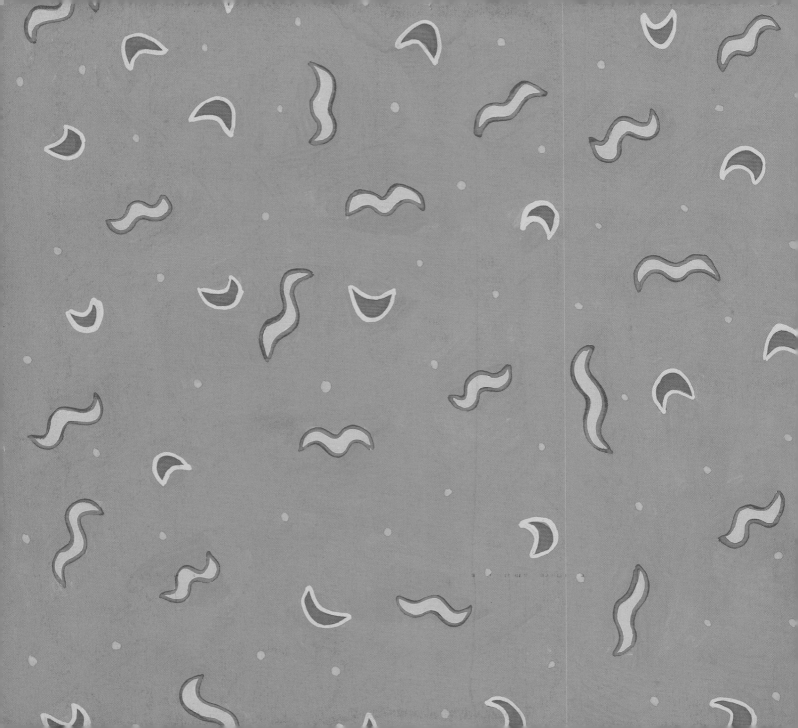

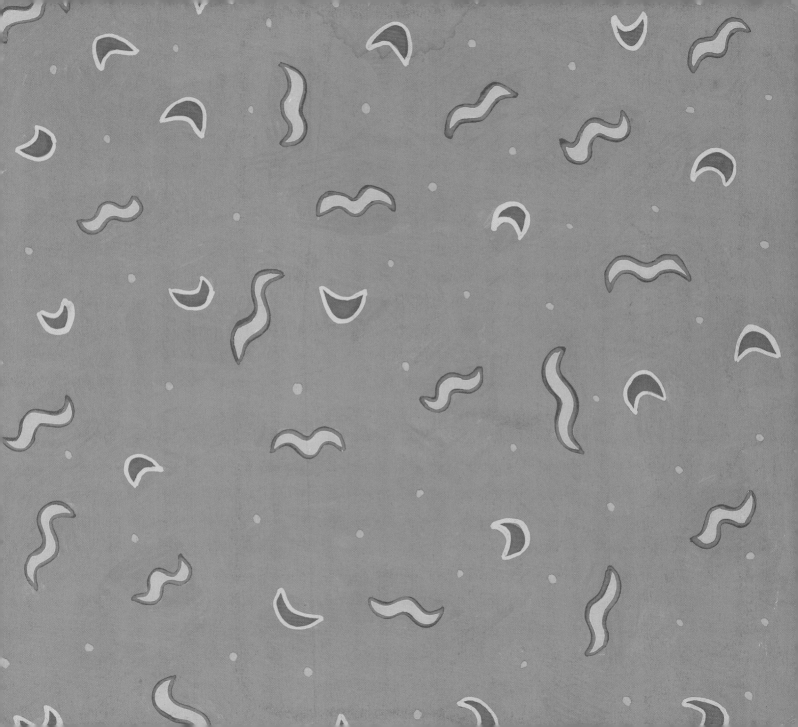

SALLY MORGAN, both a visual artist and a writer, has written books for both children and adults. Her autobiography, *My Place*, is an Australian classic. Her work as an artist has won international acclaim and is represented in galleries worldwide. Sally is a descendant of the Palyku people of the Pilbara in Western Australia; she has three children (Blaze Kwaymullina is one of them) and lives in Perth, Western Australia.

BLAZE JAKE KWAYMULLINA is a children's writer and also works in the sphere of storytelling. Blaze runs his own digital media company, Kaarunga Media. In his spare time he likes reading, rock-climbing, yoga and taking his dog Chris swimming at the local dog beach. Blaze lives in Perth, Western Australia.